RAMBLING TED™

Rambling Ted's
Terrible Mix-Up

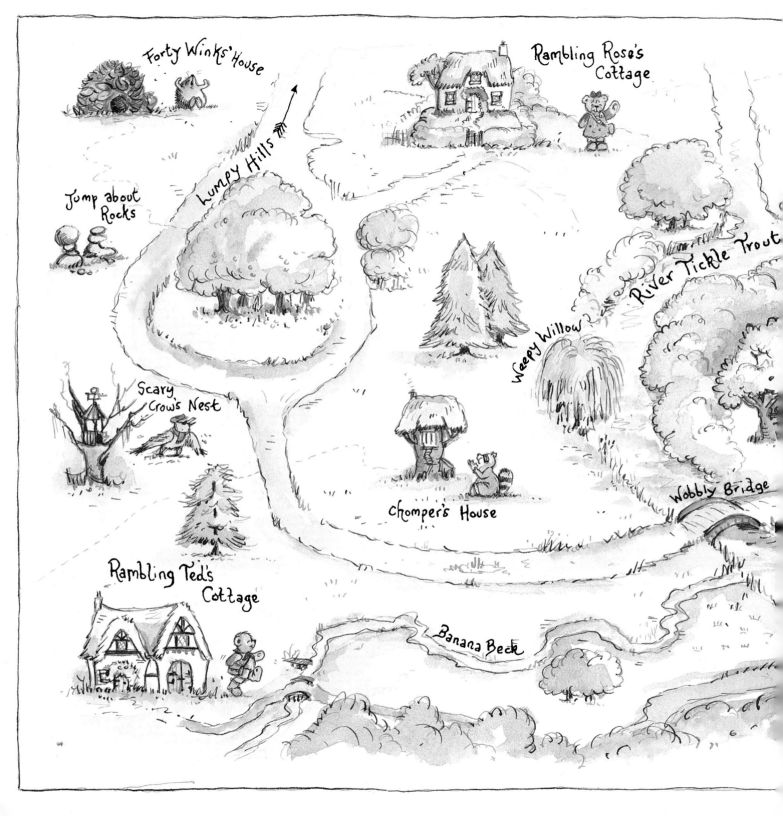

Forty Winks' House

Rambling Rose's Cottage

Lumpy Hills

Jump about Rocks

River Tickle Trout

Weepy Willow

Scary Crow's Nest

Chomper's House

Wobbly Bridge

Rambling Ted's Cottage

Banana Beck

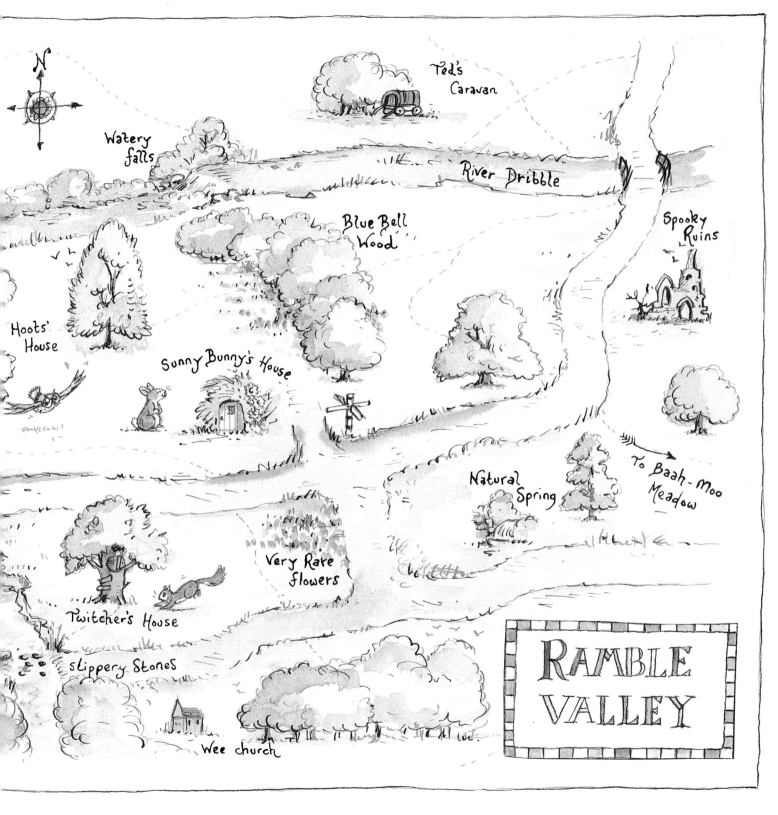

N

Ted's
Caravan

Watery
falls

River Dribble

Blue Bell
Wood

Spooky
Ruins

Hoots'
House

Sunny Bunny's House

Natural
Spring

To Baah-
Moo
Meadow

Very Rare
Flowers

Twitcher's House

Slippery Stones

Wee church

RAMBLE
VALLEY

For my wife, Mandy Abrams with love. M.A.

First published in Great Britain by HarperCollins*Publishers* Ltd in 2000
1 3 5 7 9 10 8 6 4 2
ISBN: 0 00 664700 6
Text copyright © Lindsay Camp 2000
Illustrations copyright © Michael Abrams 2000
© 1999 Michael Woodward Creations created by Michael Abrams
Rambling Ted was created and illustrated by Michael Abrams.
Rambling Ted trademark is owned by Michael Woodward Creations.
The author and illustrator assert the moral right to be identified
as the author and illustrator of the work.

The HarperCollins website address is:
www.**fire**and**water**.com

Printed and bound in Singapore.

Rambling Ted's
Terrible Mix-Up

written by Lindsay Camp
illustrated by Michael Abrams

PictureLions
An Imprint of HarperCollins*Publishers*

It was getting late, but in the kitchen at The Rosary, Rose was hard at work. She was making some of her famous mixtures.

Whenever her friends in Ramble Valley had any aches or pains, Rose would hunt high and low for just the right herbs and plants to make them better.

Tonight, she was making a special Alertness Ointment for Forty Winks the hedgehog, who was always dropping off to sleep at the most inconvenient moments.

And for Twitcher the squirrel – well, he had the same problem as Forty Winks, only backwards. He spent so much time worrying about everything, that he couldn't sleep a wink. So Rose was making him some Drowsiness Droplets to sprinkle on his pillow.

Just as Rose was finishing, there was a gentle tapping at the window.

"Ted!" said Rose, opening the kitchen door. "Whatever are you doing out this late?"

"Well," said Ted, "I went for a ramble in the Lumpy Hills and—"

"Let me guess," laughed Rose. "You got lost?"

Ted looked sheepish. For a country bear who loved going on long rambles, he didn't have a very good sense of direction.

"Not exactly lost," he said. "I just wasn't quite sure which was the best way home – and then I saw the light in your window…"

As he was leaving, Ted had an idea.

"I know," he said. "I could deliver your mixtures to Twitcher and Forty Winks on my way home. It'd be no trouble."

"Thank you, Ted," said Rose, a bit doubtfully. "But make sure you get them the right way round – the red jar is for Twitcher, and the blue one is for Forty Winks."

Ted set off, repeating to himself, "Red for Twitcher, blue for Forty Winks… red for Twitcher, blue for Forty Winks…"

And then he thought of a rhyme to help him remember. "Twitcher's jar is red because he needs to go to bed, For Forty Winks the blue, because he's got so much to do."

It was very late now, so when Ted came to The Wormery he decided to leave the jar on the doorstep. He was quite sure that inside, Forty Winks would be curled up in a loudly snoring ball.

And he did the same at The Doomery,
where Twitcher lived, just in case the
gloomy little squirrel had managed to fall asleep.

Then, tired out after this long ramble, Ted hurried straight home to bed.

But back at The Rosary, Rose was worried. What if Ted had mixed up the jars? He was very kind, but he did get confused rather easily.

It was no good, she'd have to go and check…

S ure enough, when she arrived at The Wormery, a little out of breath, there was her red jar on Forty Winks's doorstep.

Lucky I came, thought Rose. And she quickly ran to The Doomery, and switched the jars round.

Meanwhile, Ted couldn't sleep.
"This isn't like me," he thought,
as he tossed and turned in bed.

"Maybe I need some of Twitcher's
Drowsiness Droplets…"

Then, in a flash, it came back to him: Twitcher's jar is red because he needs to go to bed. He'd got it wrong! Foolish bear!

Thank goodness there was time to put it right before Twitcher and Forty Winks woke up.

Pulling on his boots, Ted was on his way.

ut when he arrived, panting, at The Wormery, Ted was very puzzled. There on the doorstep was a blue jar.

Ted scratched his head. Somehow he knew he'd got it wrong.

He always got things like that wrong. So it must have been blue for Twitcher, red for Forty Winks…

Yes, that must have been it, thought Ted, switching the jars round and going back home to bed.

Very, very early next morning, somebody else noticed the jars on the doorsteps.

It was Scary Crow. Flying over Ramble Valley, looking for mischief, his beady eyes spied a blue jar outside the Doomery, a red one on the doorstep of the Wormery.

"Aha! Young Rose's mixtures," he muttered to himself. "Maybe I'll do a little mixing myself…"

A little later, Ted was just finishing his breakfast, when Rose called round.

"You'll never guess what I did last night," said Ted.

"I think I will," smiled Rose. "You mixed up the jars. But it's all right, I switched them round."

"But so did I," gasped Ted. "That means…"

"Quick!" said Rose. "We'd better run."

Outside The Wormery, Forty Winks
was inspecting his worm store.
"Good morning!" he called brightly.
"Out for an early morning jog, are
we? Very good for you, I'm sure."
Rose and Ted were out of breath.

"That reminds me," Forty Winks went on. "Thanks most kindly for the ointment, Rose. Don't know when I felt this frisky!"

"But–" said Rose and Ted together, still panting slightly.

"Fancy a worm?" asked Forty Winks.

And, watching through his telescope, Scary Crow wondered how his mixture mix-up could possibly have gone wrong.

zzzZZZ

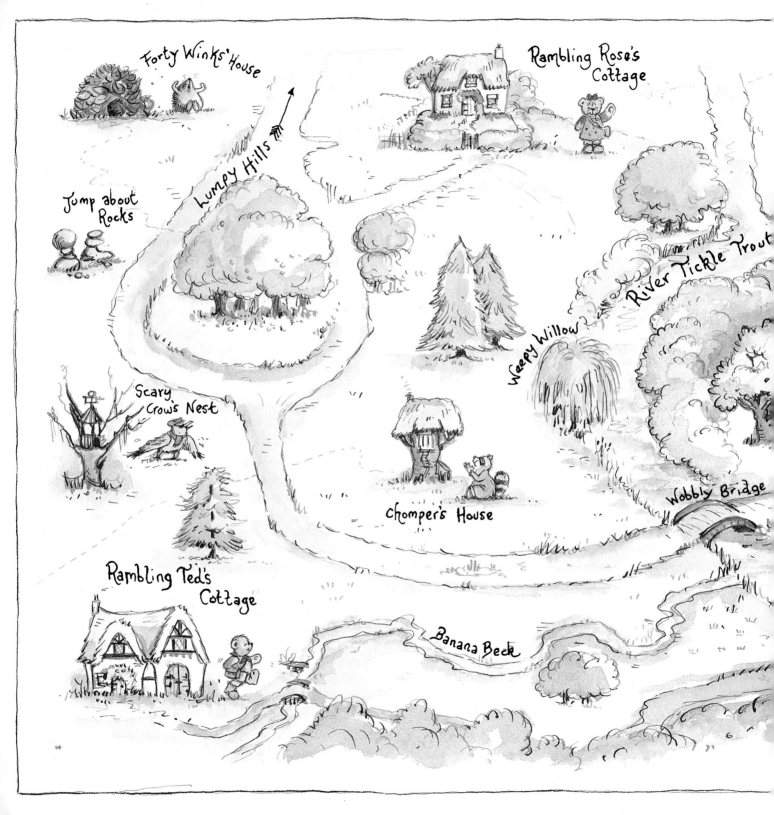

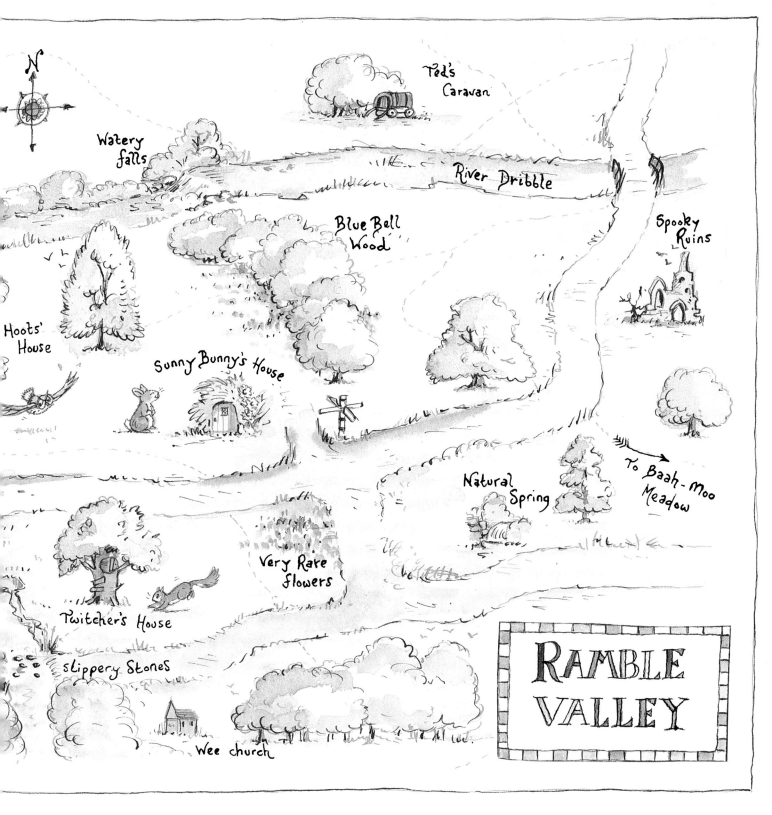